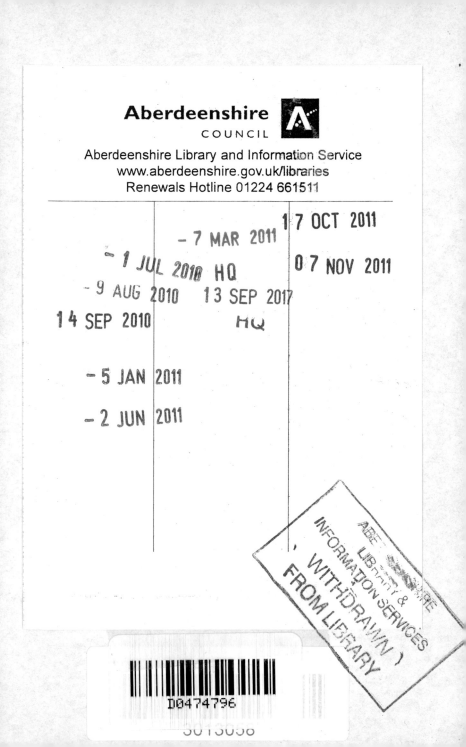

FOR ALEXANDRA HEYWOOD AND HER
FRIENDS AT THE CHINA-BRITAIN
BUSINESS COUNCIL WHO WERE SO
HELPFUL AND PATIENT WITH OUR
QUESTIONS - JB & SV

STRIPES PUBLISHING
An imprint of Magi Publications
1 The Coda Centre, 189 Munster Road,
London SW6 6AW

A paperback original
First published in Great Britain in 2009

Text copyright © Jan Burchett and Sara Vogler, 2009
Illustrations copyright © Diane Le Feyer of Cartoon Saloon, 2009
Cover illustration copyright © Andrew Hutchinson, 2009

ISBN: 978-1-84715-053-0

A CIP catalogue record for this book is available
from the British Library.

Printed and bound in Germany.

10 9 8 7 6 5 4 3 2 1

WILD RESCUE

EARTHQUAKE ESCAPE

J. Burchett and S. Vogler

STATUS: LIVE
LOCATION:
SICHUAN, CHINA
CODE NAME: JING JING

STATUS: FILE CLOSED
LOCATION:
SUMATRA, INDONESIA
CODE NAME: TORA

RESCUE
MISSION DATABASE

CHAPTER ONE

"Wahoo!" yelled Ben as he hit the top of
the hill and freewheeled in mid-air.

He hit the ground hard and risked a quick
look back at his twin sister Zoe. She was
catching up. Their mountain bikes were
new – a present from their gran – and a race
across this remote hillside was a perfect way
to try them out.

Pedalling faster, Ben swerved round a
tree root and skidded on a patch of mud,
only just keeping his balance. As Ben
righted himself, Zoe took the opportunity

to overtake. She pelted off down the steep slope. The shallow stream at the bottom was their finishing line, next to which Gran was sitting in her car, reading a book.

Gran had come to live with them during the summer holidays while their parents were away. Mr and Mrs Woodward were vets whose work took them all round the world. Usually Ben and Zoe went with them, but in September they'd be starting secondary school, so this summer they were staying at home.

Whooping triumphantly, Zoe splashed through the stream.

"The winner!" she cried.

"You wait till next time," a mud-splattered Ben grinned as he zoomed up behind her. "You were just lucky…"

He stopped. Directly overhead they heard the whir of a helicopter and the nearby trees swayed from side to side. They looked up in surprise. The next instant two harnesses on ropes flapped down just in front of them.

"What's going on?" asked Ben.

"I recognize that chopper!" yelled Zoe in delight. "Looks like Uncle Stephen wants us."

Ben and Zoe's godfather, Dr Stephen Fisher, ran a top secret organization called Wild. It was dedicated to rescuing endangered animals all over the world – and Ben and Zoe were its youngest operatives.

"Better get up there and see what mission he has for us this time!" said Ben, seizing one of the harnesses and strapping himself securely in. Soon they were being hoisted high above the trees.

Zoe gave a gasp. "What about our bikes?" she yelled over the deafening sound of the blades.

Ben looked down and waved at a small figure on the ground. "Gran's got that in hand," he yelled back. "She knows what we're up to before we do ourselves!"

"Good morning," said the pilot, as Ben and Zoe settled themselves inside the helicopter. "As you can guess, your godfather has another job for you."

"Where's he sending us, Erika?" asked Zoe, pulling on her headset and wrinkling her nose at the familiar smell of the engine. Dr Fisher had designed the helicopter to run on chicken manure – environmentally friendly, but very smelly.

"I can't tell you that." Erika smiled as she passed them an envelope. Although the young German woman was Dr Fisher's second-in-command, and had all the information at her fingertips, she knew their eccentric godfather would want to explain their mission himself.

"I bet I know what's in here," said Ben. He plunged his hand into the envelope. "A glass eye."

"Our clue to the next rescue mission," exclaimed Zoe, studying it. "But which animal has eyes like this? It's got a slit pupil."

"Alligator?" suggested Ben. "Snake?"

"There's one simple way to find out," Erika told them. "It fits in that console over there."

Ben placed the eye into a small hollow between some coloured switches and at once a hologram of a man in a Hawaiian shirt appeared. He had a bowler hat shoved over his thick red hair.

"Greetings, godchildren," he boomed. "Brief message. Sending you to China. A giant panda cub's in trouble. Full details when you arrive." The image faded.

"A giant panda," beamed Zoe. "They're the cutest things."

"Not so cute if it sat on you," snorted Ben. "A fully grown one weighs more than a hundred kilograms. They have to eat for about fifteen hours a day just to stay alive."

"Sounds like you!" Zoe laughed.

"And they're seriously endangered," added Ben, ignoring her. "Their main diet's bamboo and lots of bamboo forests have been cut down."

"I knew that, Mr Factfile!" said Zoe.

"Well, you didn't know they have slit pupils," said Ben.

"Neither did you!" retorted Zoe.

Soon they'd left the land behind and headed north across the choppy sea to

Uncle Stephen's remote island. As soon as they'd landed and climbed out, Erika activated the mechanism that brought up the fake shed to hide the helicopter. Zoe and Ben ran over to a decrepit outside toilet.

Zoe flung open the tatty door and they all crammed in.

"Hold on to your stomachs!" joked Ben, as the toilet became a secret turbo lift and sped deep underground.

Ben and Zoe hurried along the brightly-lit corridor and placed their fingertips on an ID pad next to a door marked Control Room.

"Print identification complete," came an electronic voice.

The door slid open and Ben and Zoe burst into the huge room with its high-tech plasma screens all over the walls.

Uncle Stephen swung round in his chair, a look of delight on his face. "That was

quick!" he beamed. "Glad to see you're as
keen as ever."

"Tell us about the panda," said Zoe,
eagerly. "How can we help?"

Uncle Stephen led them over to the
largest screen. He touched it and brought
up an image of a solemn panda cub sitting
on a tree stump. "This is Jing Jing."

"Adorable!" gushed Zoe.

Ben raised his eyebrows. "She's gone into Gooey Heaven," he groaned. Ben was as fond of animals as his sister, but there were times when she just got too slushy for words.

The image changed to a satellite map of China and zoomed in on a thickly wooded mountainous region. In a valley formed by a river gorge were a group of buildings and fenced areas. The mountains rose up steeply on either side.

"Jing Jing lives here at the Ningshang Sanctuary." Erika joined in the briefing. "It's in Sichuan Province in the west of China."

"Wasn't there an earthquake there last month?" asked Zoe.

"Indeed there was, Zoe," said Dr Fisher. "And the sanctuary was badly damaged. Luckily there weren't too many casualties – and all the pandas were saved – but there's been a lot of rebuilding needed."

Erika touched the screen toolbar and the

image changed to a video clip of young pandas slowly clambering up a climbing frame. "We don't have any footage of Jing Jing," she told them, "but here are some other one-year-old panda cubs in the kindergarten compound. They're orphans and have lived there most of their lives. Pandas aren't really independent until they're two and able to forage for themselves. Only then are they released into the wild."

"They're like clumsy little teddy bears," said Zoe, looking at the cubs as they tumbled down a slide.

"Since the earthquake in Sichuan Province, Wild has been particularly concerned for the safety of the animals there," Erika went on. "We've put the area on red alert. We thought the sanctuary pandas would be fine. But five days ago we got news that Jing Jing was missing. He'd escaped through a small break in the fencing of his compound. It was damaged in an aftershock."

"Did the sanctuary send out a search party?" asked Zoe.

"Certainly," said Uncle Stephen. "They're a dedicated team at Ningshang. But they found no sign of him and had to give up. They haven't got enough workers there to spare for such a task."

Ben nodded. "I suppose they must still be repairing all the damage and trying to keep all the other pandas safe."

"You're right," said Erika. "And aftershocks are undoing some of the rebuilding work. Everyone out there is struggling to get things back to normal."

"If Jing Jing's too young to forage he won't last long on his own," said Zoe, worried.

"And he'll be very scared," added Uncle Stephen.

"Then we'd better get to China as soon as we can," declared Ben. "Let's get packed!"

"I knew I could rely on my godchildren," said Uncle Stephen, delighted. "But you can't go without these." He rummaged in a messy drawer in his desk and pulled out what looked like two sleek hand-held games consoles. "Your BUGs!" He handed them to Ben and Zoe.

The BUGs, or Brilliant Undercover Gizmos, were incredibly clever. They could be used to communicate with Wild HQ, track animals, translate languages and tons of other stuff as well. Ben and Zoe still hadn't found out half the things they could do.

"And you might want these," said Uncle Stephen. "They'll prove useful in the mountains." He handed them a couple of slim torches. "These are my FINs – Fisher Integrated Nanofirers."

"A new invention?" gasped Ben. "What does it do? I want to try it now."

"Not in here!" said Erika quickly. "It's designed for the outdoors. I'll tell you all about it in the plane to China. Now, let's get you kitted out. Dr Fisher has been busy inventing things. Here are some thermogoggles for tracking animals by heat. You'll have fun with these," she said, as she handed them over. "And we've got some new reinforced backpacks we want you to try out."

"Remember it's dangerous terrain in those mountains at the best of times," Uncle Stephen warned them. "There may still be aftershocks. They can occur up to a year after a quake. Make sure you keep yourselves safe. Remember if you feel one coming – drop to the ground and cover your head!"

"I'll give you a demonstration on Wild's new earthquake simulator," said Erika.

"Cool!" exclaimed Ben.

"Then you'll be prepared if you face that danger," Erika went on.

Zoe and Ben exchanged glances. They each knew what the other was thinking. They never looked for danger, but danger seemed to find them!

CHAPTER TWO

Ben flung open the bedroom window and gazed up at the densely wooded mountain slopes that stretched away as far as the eye could see.

"I can't wait to start our search for Jing Jing," he said eagerly as he pulled on his boots. "Let's get into that forest."

Ben and Zoe had arrived the previous day in China at a private airfield outside Chengdu. From there Erika had driven them over cracked and potholed Sichuan roads to the little village that lay in a deep

valley next to a fast-flowing river. It had
been very late when they arrived at the
Panda Palace Hotel – a simple guest house
that had been damaged by the earthquake.
Part of its roof was missing and only one
bathroom was in use but the owner, Yao
Zhi, had given them a warm welcome,
although he looked surprised to have guests
so soon after the earthquake.

"Jing Jing could be anywhere," said Zoe,
picking up her new backpack. "If you
charge off straight away I'll be sending a
search party out for you!"

"I know we agreed to go to the sanctuary
first." Ben stuffed his BUG into his pocket.
"But suppose we don't get any useful
information – we'll have wasted time."

"The workers there know him well,"
insisted Zoe. "We should be able to find out
about any distinctive characteristics,
favourite food, that type of thing."

"As long as we don't let on why we want to know," warned Ben, fidgeting at the door as he waited for Zoe to follow. "Remember, we're just normal holiday makers…"

"…come to see the pandas," said Zoe, finishing his sentence. She grabbed their waterproof jackets from the little wardrobe. "We're sure to need these. Erika said it can rain at any time here."

"And we'd better warn the guest house owner that we might not be back tonight," suggested Ben.

"Good thinking!" said Zoe. "We have no idea where the search will take us and we don't want him thinking we're lost."

Downstairs Ben handed the room key to Mr Zhi at reception.

"I hope you enjoyed your breakfast," Mr Zhi said. He spoke good English – Erika had told them the local people were used to tourists.

"Delicious!" said Ben with a grin, remembering the tasty steamed buns filled with lamb and served with rice porridge. "The baozi was the best."

"Your aunt left early today," Mr Zhi went on. "You were still asleep I think."

"Aunt Erika has some work in Chengdu," Zoe explained quickly. "We're used to her going off. We're quite happy on our own."

The hotel owner looked disapproving but he said nothing.

Ben and Zoe had to be careful that no one suspected the real reason why two children were left on their own in a foreign country. Everyone had to believe that they were on holiday with their eccentric aunt. Erika had actually gone off to another devastated area to check on the wildlife there.

"We're going to visit the Ningshang Panda Sanctuary," Zoe told him. "I've always wanted to see giant pandas."

"Just like all the tourists!" Mr Zhi smiled in relief. "You'll be safe there without your aunt."

"She's meeting us there later," said Ben. "She wants to take us on an outing. We'll be away for the night but probably back tomorrow."

Mr Zhi nodded. "Where are you going?"

"We don't know," said Zoe hurriedly. "It's a surprise."

"Wait for a moment. I'll give you a packed lunch."

Mr Zhi was soon back carrying two paper bags that bulged with stuffed pancakes.

Ben's eyes lit up. "Thanks," he said, putting them into his backpack.

Zoe and Ben followed the river out of the village towards the sanctuary, walking over cracked, rubble-strewn ground. Either side of the road were half-collapsed buildings, some with curtains still hanging from broken windows.

Builders were clearing and demolishing, calling to each other in Chinese.

"Better put in our translators," Ben reminded Zoe, struggling to pull out the squidgy little earpiece from the side of his BUG. "What did Erika say they speak round here?"

"Sichuanese." Zoe pressed hers into her ear and listened to the banter. "That's interesting," she said with a grin. "They're saying, 'Who's that ugly-looking boy over the road?'"

Ben quickly shoved his earpiece in.

"No they're not!" he declared. "They're
moaning about the local football scores."

"Got you!" Zoe laughed, running off
before he could get his revenge.

They came to the remains of a bus shelter
that had fallen into a deep hole.

"It must have been really
frightening when the earthquake hit,"
said Ben soberly. "That simulation we
went in at Wild HQ was bad enough."

"It would be terrifying for the
pandas," added Zoe with a
shudder. "They wouldn't have
understood what was happening."

The winding road led away from
the houses and soon the high
wooden fence of the sanctuary came
into view. Behind it loomed the
densely forested mountains. Clouds
hung low around the
peaks in a thick mist.

"Look over there," said Ben, pointing to where the tree line began. "That land used to be forest but it's all been cleared. We saw a lot of that on the way here with Erika."

"Something's being built," said Zoe. "Poor pandas, losing their home. It's terrible when people don't think of the animal life."

Ben brought up a satellite map of the area on his BUG and zoomed in on the Ningshang Sanctuary.

"It's bigger than I thought," he said, showing Zoe. "Like a large park in England."

"But where do the wild pandas live?" asked Zoe. "I reckon that's where Jing Jing's most likely to have gone."

"I read all about it on the plane journey," Ben explained. "So much of the bamboo forest has been cut down that there are only pockets here and there. The wild pandas have become quite isolated in their own little areas. Although there are a few places in Sichuan where the government and conservation groups have planted bamboo corridors to join these up."

"That doesn't help us," said Zoe, looking at the scattered zones of bamboo on the screen. "Jing Jing could be anywhere.

He's had plenty of time! Erika said he'd been missing five days, six now. I just hope he's found a bamboo forest."

They arrived at the wooden gates of the sanctuary. It appeared open but no one was sitting at the ticket booth. They could hear Chinese voices and the sound of hammering and sawing.

"I can't see any tourists," said Zoe, peering round, worried. "I hope it's open."

"Can I help you?" said a voice in English.

A Chinese man in a white coat was approaching. There was a solemn young girl with him who stared at them from under a thick fringe of shiny dark hair. She wore a blue sweatshirt with a panda logo. She looked about seven.

"We'd like to see round the sanctuary please," said Zoe. "Is that possible?"

"Our guides are all busy," said the man, with an apologetic shrug. "They're doing repair work. I don't like to turn visitors away, but I'm afraid there can be no tours today."

"I can show them round, Father," said the girl, pulling at his sleeve. She spoke in Sichuanese and Zoe and Ben had to pretend they hadn't understood. "We won't get in the way, I promise," the little girl went on.

"I don't think it's a good idea," replied the man, also in his own language. "We're in such confusion here."

Ben and Zoe had no choice but to turn and walk away, desperately hoping the man would agree with his daughter before they had gone too far. "Walk slowly," muttered Ben.

"Go on, Father," they heard the little girl beg.

The man sighed. "Wait a minute, please," he called in English. Ben and Zoe spun round. "My daughter, Xu Mei, knows a lot about what we do here and will show you round. There will be no charge, of course."

"Thank you so much!" cried Ben and Zoe, running back eagerly.

"That's settled then," said the man. He patted his daughter on the head and went off to one of the buildings.

"Come with me, please," said Xu Mei in English, grinning broadly.

"You speak our language very well," said Zoe.

"I learn it at school," said Xu Mei. "What are your names?"

"She's Zoe and I'm Ben."

Xu Mei gave them a small polite nod, then led them between two grey stone buildings into a courtyard. People in blue sanctuary sweatshirts were carrying buckets of vegetables and planks of wood about. They smiled at the children and carried on with their jobs.

"This is the visitors' area," said Xu Mei, with a sweep of her arm. "Here's the café and the gift shop, and over there is the information office."

A red banner with some gold Chinese characters hung over the open door that Xu Mei was pointing to. 'Find out all about our pandas', it said in English underneath. Through the doorway they could see a large, brightly lit room. Inside, display boards showed photographs and descriptions of life at the sanctuary.

"And there is the enclosure for the panda cubs." She smiled shyly at them and nodded towards a solid wooden fence. "That's my favourite place."

Zoe raced across the courtyard and looked eagerly over the fence. The grassy

compound beyond was much lower than the
courtyard. There were wooden huts around
the edge with small entry doors and what
looked like a child's climbing frame in the
centre. A group of young pandas was playing
on it, tumbling slowly over each other, biting
each other's ears and paws. Others were
lumbering about on the grass, or lazing on
their backs, chewing bamboo.

"I'd love to go in and just hug them!"
breathed Zoe.

"You could be their mummy!" teased Ben.

"They do need a mother," said Xu Mei
earnestly. "They are all … what is the word
… orphans. They are just the same as little
children. People think they like to live
alone but these little ones are very friendly
– with each other and their keepers. I even
go in and play sometimes – when a grown-up
is there."

Zoe looked enviously at her.

"That's bamboo, isn't it?" said Ben,
pointing at a little thicket of tall, waving
plants in the corner, "and I can see you give
them vegetables. I've read all about it.
They're given vitamins, rice, honey, carrots
and apples. And a special bread."

"We give them milk as well," Xu Mei told
them. "In bottles just like babies have.
They grow much bigger than pandas in the

wild. Wild pandas have to eat bamboo all day just to get enough goodness."

"Did all your pandas survive the earthquake?" asked Zoe, with a glance at Ben. She knew they mustn't admit they already knew about the lost panda. They had to hear it from Xu Mei. Keeping Wild a secret made things difficult at times.

"Yes," said their guide, "but they were very scared and some of the buildings fell down." Her face fell. "Then last week one of the panda cubs escaped from here. The fence got broken by an aftershock, you see."

"Oh dear," said Ben gently. "Has it been found?"

Xu Mei shook her head. "We all searched for him but we have no more time now. He was my favourite." Her eyes filled with tears. "There are clouded leopards in the forest. My father has seen one attack a wild panda there. Jing Jing is in big danger."

CHAPTER THREE

"That's terrible," said Zoe. "Do you have any idea where he went?"

At that Xu Mei began to cry, her body shaking with sobs. Zoe felt awful. They needed to find out all they could about Jing Jing, but she had never meant to upset the little girl like this.

She put her arm round her. "Would you show us the rest of the sanctuary?" she said. "We'd really like that and it might cheer you up. You're a very good guide."

Xu Mei gulped and wiped her eyes.

Zoe took her hand and led her towards the information office.

"Let's look in here," she said.

"What are you doing?" whispered Ben, following them in. "I know it's a great place, but if we're going to find out about Jing Jing— "

"Got an idea," Zoe whispered back.

Ben shrugged. There were times when he just had to trust that his sister knew what she was doing. He wandered around, absorbing as much information as he could about panda habits.

Zoe quickly scanned the photos on display for a picture of Jing Jing. There were tiny pink pandas in incubators, mothers with their cubs and a whole board of photos of young panda cubs sleeping and eating and playing. None of the names underneath were Jing Jing's.

Then her gaze stopped at a picture on a

wall-mounted board. It
was the photo of a young
girl cuddling a tiny baby
panda and feeding it
from a bottle. It was so
young that its markings
were only just
beginning to show

through its fuzzy white fur. "That's you,
isn't it?" she asked Xu Mei, who was
following her silently round the display.
"And the panda?" she added.

"Jing Jing," Xu Mei said, almost in a
whisper. "He is the one who is lost."

She pointed to the next photo. It showed
a line of tubby panda cubs with their noses
deep in their feeding bowls. "Jing Jing is the
one at the end," she explained. "He is
trying to eat his friend's dinner."

"And this one is me with Jing Jing," Xu
Mei said, smiling sadly.

"He is much bigger now," she explained. "He is one. He was only a few days old when my father found him in the wild. He was with his mother, but she was dead. He was half underneath her and his back paw was squashed. The one on the left. It's a funny shape now and two claws are missing."

Ben gave Zoe a secret thumbs up as Xu Mei moved along the display. This must be Zoe's way of getting the information they needed – and it seemed to be working.

"What had happened to his mother?" asked Ben.

"She had not got enough food," said Xu Mei. "The bamboo where she was living had died."

"It was lucky your father found Jing Jing when he did," said Zoe.

"I do not think Jing Jing will be so lucky this time," said Xu Mei desperately. "He cannot live for long on his own in the wild.

He will not know what to do to eat and
how to keep safe. He might not find any
bamboo. I wanted to go and search for him
but my father said no, it is too dangerous for
me in the mountains. Remember the
leopards I told you about." A tear ran down
her cheek. "Poor little Jing Jing. I hope he
doesn't meet one."

Zoe took her hand.
"Supposing we look
for him," she said.
"Ben and I, I mean."

Xu Mei stared at her
with sudden
hope in
her eyes.

"You can do that?" she said. Then she shook her head. "But how? You do not know these mountains."

"Jing Jing may not have got that far," explained Ben. "He could be hiding somewhere close by, too terrified to move."

For the first time Xu Mei's face broke into a smile. "Then I will come with you. I will get some of Jing Jing's food for us to take, and a feeding bottle. He will be so hungry." She darted out of the door.

When she had gone, Zoe gently stroked the photo of the tiny panda cub lying in Xu Mei's arms, his little pink mouth guzzling at the bottle.

"I hope we can find him." She sighed. "It's not going to be easy."

"Xu Mei is relying on us – and so is Jing Jing," said Ben firmly. "We can't let them down."

CHAPTER FOUR

"So this is where Jing Jing got out." Ben bent down at the side of the road to examine the boarded-up area of fencing. After returning with some panda food and a bottle, which Ben and Zoe stowed safely in their backpacks, Xu Mei had led them out of the sanctuary and straight to Jing Jing's escape route.

"He must have squeezed through," said Zoe. "Did he leave any paw prints?"

Xu Mei shrugged. "Lots of people were around and the ground got all messed up.

We couldn't find any."

Zoe turned away from the sanctuary fence and looked at the land beyond. In the distance she could see water glinting off the rice fields. Just on the other side of the road was a cluster of low buildings and people working in the fields amongst a sea of waving yellow stalks.

"I recognize that crop," said Zoe. "It's wheat, nearly full grown. Would Jing Jing eat that?"

Xu Mei shook her head. "He wouldn't like it," she said. "He would have kept on going – and he would soon be lost."

"But supposing he didn't," said Ben suddenly. "What if he got scared and hid in a barn or something? He could be there now."

"Don't be daft," scoffed Zoe. "The sanctuary will have told everyone to be on the look out for Jing Jing. The farmer must have searched for him already."

"He says he has but I think he has been too busy since the earthquake," said Xu Mei.

"So it's possible that Jing Jing is hiding on the farm!" said Ben.

Xu Mei nodded eagerly.

"Let's ask the farmer if we can search," suggested Zoe.

"Mr Chen is a bit grumpy," said Xu Mei, "and he does not speak English."

"Then it's lucky you're with us." Ben grinned.

The three children walked along a wide track past a ramshackle barn. Zoe peered in, hoping to catch sight of the little panda. She got a quick glimpse of a pile of empty sacks and some straw before they moved on.

At last they reached the single storey farmhouse and stood uncertainly under the corrugated metal sheet which overhung Mr Chen's front door. They could hear the sounds

of noisy chickens from behind the house.
The untidy yard was full of ladders, piles of
wood and broken bricks. The ground all around
was cracked and pitted from the earthquake.
A dog barked from somewhere nearby.

"Still got your translation earpiece in?"
Zoe whispered to her brother.

"You bet."

"Remember we mustn't show we
understand," Zoe reminded him in an
undertone.

The door was flung open at Xu Mei's timid
knock. Mr Chen was a solemn man, and he
didn't look pleased at being disturbed.

"I know you!" He spoke rapidly in
Sichuanese to the little girl. "You come
from that sanctuary. What do you want?"

The translated voice was crystal clear
through the BUG earpieces.

"I am so sorry to trouble you, sir," Xu
Mei said quietly, "and I hope you will

forgive me." She looked at the ground as she spoke.

Zoe was glad that it was not her and Ben negotiating. They knew so little about Chinese manners, which seemed so different from their own.

"We are trying to find the panda that got lost," Xu Mei went on in a rush. "We would be so happy if you would let us look in your barn."

Mr Chen sniffed. "If you have time to waste. I haven't seen it there."

All of a sudden, there was a faint rumbling sound and the ground beneath them vibrated for a few seconds. They flexed their knees against the movement to keep their balance.

Ben and Zoe looked at each other.

"Aftershock!"

Dust showered down from the farmhouse roof. A piece of tin sheeting slipped down and hung at a dangerous angle.

Mr Chen waved them away impatiently.
"Even more work for me now. Off you go."

Xu Mei bowed her head politely and
walked away. Ben and Zoe did the same.

"He says we can look in his barn," said
Xu Mei.

They hurried over. Broken boxes and rusty tools lay about the floor. At the back straw bales were stacked high against the wall. Ben began to poke about amongst some broken machinery in a corner while Xu Mei climbed up the mountain of bales.

"Nothing here," she called down.

Zoe helped Ben ferret among the bits of rusting metal. "Wait!" she said suddenly. "What's that? Behind the thing with the prongs. I can see white fur."

There was a movement among the dark shadows. Ben got a torch out of his backpack and shone it into the corner. Xu Mei immediately leaped down to join them. She dropped to her hands and knees and wriggled under the dirty machinery.

"Jing Jing!" she called softly.

"Yowwwwl!"

A scrawny white cat shot past her outstretched hand and disappeared behind the straw.

"I'm so sorry," said Zoe. "I got your hopes up for nothing. I don't think Jing Jing can be here, Xu Mei. We'd better—"

She stopped. Behind them something had come into the barn. Then there was a terrifying sound that made the hairs on the back of their necks stand up on end.

CHAPTER FIVE

A deep, threatening growl filled the barn.
The children turned slowly to see a guard
dog in the doorway, teeth bared. It was
squarely built and strong – and it looked
angry.

"Back off, everybody," muttered Ben out
of the side of his mouth. "But no sudden
movements."

"And don't look it in the eye," added Zoe.

Keeping their gaze lowered, the three
children shuffled backwards until they felt
the sharp stalks of straw against their legs.

The dog advanced, snarling all the time, its heavy chain dragging behind.

"Good thing it's tied up," said Ben. "I don't think it can reach us."

"Yes it can," wailed Xu Mei.

At the end of the chain a stake was being dragged across the ground.

"It must have come loose in the aftershock," gasped Zoe. "Climb – as fast as you can!"

Turning in an instant, they scrambled up the straw mountain. The dog lunged, snapping at the air beneath their feet. Zoe felt its hot breath on her ankle. The dog hurled itself at the straw bales again but they were too high and it fell back, snarling.

"We're stuck!" cried Xu Mei.

Zoe peered down at the dog who was clawing away at the straw, veins standing out on his neck. He wasn't going to give up until he had his quarry.

"I don't understand," said Zoe. "It's a Shar Pei. The only ones I know are friendly family pets."

"They can be trained as guard dogs though," Ben answered. "We wouldn't stand a chance against those powerful jaws."

Xu Mei's eyes looked wide and frightened in the gloom. "What are we going to do?" she whispered.

"I can feel a breeze on my back," said Zoe suddenly. She turned to investigate. "Look, the wall's broken here. That's where the air's coming from." She hooked her fingers into the split wood and pulled. It came away with a loud crack. The guard dog rapped out a fierce bark at the sound.

"Well done, Zoe. We can squeeze through," said Ben, cautiously poking his head out. "There's a bit of a drop but we'll have to risk it."

He edged in between the shattered planks, gave a push off and disappeared from sight.

Zoe looked down. Ben had landed on a pile of twigs and small logs, ready for kindling. He beckoned silently and Zoe and Xu Mei followed him. There was no sound from the dog.

They dashed for the fence, not daring to stop until they had left the farmer's land and reached the river. After checking to make sure they hadn't been followed, they sat down to get their breath back.

"No sign of Jing Jing," said Xu Mei.

"We've only looked in one place," said Zoe. "Let's have some lunch and think about what we're going to do next. We got these from the guest house we're staying in." She pulled out the packets Mr Zhi had given them and offered one to Xu Mei.

"Delicious!" Ben sighed as he tucked into his pancake filled with vegetables and chunks of chicken. "Ahhh!" he gasped. "Spicy!" He grabbed his bottle and took huge gulps of water.

"You must be staying at the Panda Palace Hotel," said Xu Mei with her mouth full. "My friend Wen lives there. You saw the roof that fell in the earthquake? He got hurt."

"Is he all right?" asked Ben.

"He was bleeding a lot," said Xu Mei solemnly. "He is in the Chengdu Hospital. My mother said it is a pity the new medical centre is not built yet." She pointed at the stretch of deforestation Ben and Zoe had noticed earlier. "He would have got help much quicker."

"We should have realized the people here have a good reason for tearing up the forest," Ben muttered to Zoe. "We were only thinking how bad it was for the pandas."

"True," Zoe whispered back. "Chengdu is a long way to go if you're injured."

They munched away at their lunch for a few moments.

"Where shall we look now?" Xu Mei carried on, fingers wrapped firmly round a bean shoot pancake. "My father said I must not go into the mountains but I think we have to."

Zoe suddenly felt dreadfully guilty. They'd already dragged the little girl into a dangerous situation. This was their mission and they shouldn't have risked her safety. She'd never have forgiven herself if the farmer's dog had attacked Xu Mei. They would have to continue hunting on their own. She made a big show of looking at her watch.

"I don't think we have time to search any more today," she said. "Aunt Erika will be expecting us."

Ben gave her a puzzled look. "But she's—"

"Waiting," interrupted Zoe firmly. "So we have to go back to the hotel."

"Listen. I've an idea where he could be," said Xu Mei eagerly. "He could have gone back to where he was born – where my father found him." She shaded her eyes and looked at the mountain slope beyond the cleared land. "It was near a big waterfall, he said. Somewhere up there."

"I'm sorry, Xu Mei, but after meeting that dog I think we'd better leave finding Jing Jing to the grown-ups," said Zoe, ignoring Ben's look of astonishment.

Xu Mei's eyes filled with tears. "But Jing Jing needs us now. You said you would find him with me."

"Maybe tomorrow," said Zoe.

"Tomorrow will be too late." Xu Mei jumped to her feet. "I thought you were my friends!"

Before Ben and Zoe could stop her she ran off sobbing.

"What did you do that for, Zoe?" protested Ben. "Wild sent us here to search for Jing Jing, right?"

"And that's just what we're going to do," said Zoe. "I know it looked mean but it's not safe to take a seven-year-old with us. We've already led her into danger once."

Ben nodded. "See what you mean.

So what's our next step?"

"Xu Mei might be right about Jing Jing going back to his birthplace."

"Don't be silly," scoffed Ben. "He's not a salmon."

"We don't know what goes on inside an animal's head," insisted Zoe. "Anyway, it's as good a place to start as any." She pulled out her BUG and brought up an image of the area. She tapped in waterfall and pointed to the displayed map. "This has got to be it. It's the only waterfall near enough. Doesn't look too far."

"But it's a climb so it's going to take a lot longer than you think," said Ben. "Let's get going." He stuffed the remains of the lunch in his backpack and marched off in the direction of the forest. Then he stopped suddenly. "I've just thought of something."

"What?" asked Zoe.

"It was what Xu Mei said," Ben explained.

"She told us the bamboo had all died where Jing Jing was found. I've read about bamboo. Whole areas die at once and then they take years to grow back. If Jing Jing has gone there…"

"…he'll have nothing to eat!" exclaimed Zoe. "The poor thing will be starving!"

CHAPTER SIX

"Look at this, Ben." Zoe was crouched under a huge tree, amongst a carpet of long pine cones that lay scattered over the ground. "I've found tracks at last."

Ben ran over to join her. "Are they panda?" he asked wearily. "I was beginning to think we were in the wrong place."

The hour-long climb through the dense forest had been steep and exhausting with no sign of Jing Jing's tracks. Twice it had rained so hard that Ben and Zoe had been forced to take shelter. Now the light was fading and

they were still some way from the waterfall.
The air was full of the last of the birdsong,
interspersed with harsh monkey cries.

"They're definitely panda," insisted Zoe.
"This is a front paw. There are five toes
with claw marks and a pear-shaped pad.
The same as on the BUG." She held the
gizmo next to the imprint in the soft earth.

"Hang on," said Ben. He rummaged in his
backpack and pulled out their night goggles.
He put his on and at once everything was
clear – bathed in a green glow.

He bent down to inspect the ground.

"Well done, Zoe. It's hard to see in this
light without goggles," he said, handing over
her pair. "You're not as dim as you look!"

Ben gently felt the marks in the earth.
"The prints are fresh," he said. "They've
still got sharp edges so they must have been
made since the rain. Surely the panda can't
be far away."

Zoe scanned the ground.

"Here's another one," she said eagerly. "And another. The trail goes uphill – towards the waterfall."

"Is there a deformed print, like Jing Jing's?"

"Haven't found one yet," said Zoe, still searching. "But we'd better follow. It's the only lead we've got."

As they walked on through a grove of overhanging tung trees, a strange haunting cry filled the air.

"What's that?" hissed Zoe. "It's really eerie."

Ben feverishly worked his BUG identifier. "Clouded leopard," he said. "Their cry's not like other big cats. Xu Mei warned us about them. They're very rare – but very dangerous. We must be careful. They attack anything up to the size of a deer. So we'd make a good meal."

"Quick!" said Zoe. "Scent dispersers on! Then it won't detect our smell."

Ben and Zoe pressed the keys on their BUGs and they walked on, treading softly on leaves and small twigs.

"Can you hear that?" Ben listened hard. "The sound of water in the distance. We must be near the falls."

But Zoe didn't answer. She was standing in front of a clump of tall brown withered stalks sticking out at odd angles from the ground. Dead leaves and flowers hung limply from them. When she looked up she could see the sky clearly for the first time since they'd entered the forest.

"What's happened here?" she asked.

"It's dead bamboo," Ben told her. He crumbled one of the dried, shrivelled flower heads in his hand. It scattered over his boots. "This is really serious for the wild pandas."

"Do you think we've reached the area where Jing Jing was found when he was tiny?" said Zoe. "Xu Mei said there was dead bamboo all around and it was near the waterfall."

"Keep following that trail," urged Ben.

The forest twilight gradually faded to complete darkness. Ben and Zoe pushed through the thicket of sharp stalks, their boots crunching on dead wood. The trail of paw prints was getting harder to follow now. Zoe strode on ahead, keeping her eyes to the ground. Ben followed close behind. They could hear the distant waterfall.

"Wait, Zoe!" called Ben. "This looks interesting."

They squatted down beside a faint imprint in the mud.

"It's a back paw," said Zoe, in excitement, "and there's only three toes. It has to be

Jing Jing's. There must be more somewhere around here."

They poked about in the bamboo, scratching their arms on the broken twigs.

Suddenly there was a tremendous pattering above their heads and heavy rain pounded down through the leaves. They quickly pulled on their waterproofs.

"The trail's going," Zoe shouted to Ben above the din. "The rain's washing away the marks."

"Carry on the way they were heading," Ben shouted back. "It's uphill to the water and that's the most likely direction Jing Jing would have taken."

They hadn't gone far when the rain stopped. Now they could hear the waterfall pounding. Zoe suddenly stopped and picked up something from the ground.

"Look at this," she gasped. She passed Ben a withered bamboo branch. "It's got teeth marks in it. I bet that was Jing Jing, trying to find something to eat."

"We've got to find him," Ben nodded.

Zoe pushed through the last of the bamboo stalks and stood open-mouthed at the sight in front of her. A long stream of white water was thundering down from the steep rock above her head into a churning pool below. The pool looked treacherous. She shuddered as she thought of Jing Jing, hungry and thirsty, trying to drink here. He could even have fallen in and he might be too weak to swim.

Ben and Zoe moved slowly round the narrow bank, the water swirling violently in the pool below their feet. Halfway round they stepped over a narrow stream that trickled downhill away from the pool.

"Where does the rest of the water go?" Zoe shouted above the pounding. "There's loads coming over the fall but hardly any going into the stream."

"Most of it must be draining into an underground river," Ben shouted back.

He peered into the undergrowth, looking for signs of black and white fur. As he parted a clump of bamboo stems, something the size of a large dog started from the thicket and darted away in a panic.

"Only a musk deer," Ben called to his sister. "No antlers – and did you see those long tusks?! It was a male. The females—"

"Save the lecture till later," Zoe told him. "Keep your mind on the panda hunt."

She suddenly caught Ben's arm. "There's something moving over there," she hissed, pointing into the darkness. "See? By the fallen tree trunk."

Something was shuffling slowly among the small, craggy rocks scattered in the undergrowth a little way from the pool. Through their goggles they could just make out the occasional flash of light markings.

The shape stopped and plopped to the ground.

"It's a panda!" whispered Ben. "I caught a glimpse of a black eye patch."

"It's got to be Jing Jing!" exclaimed Zoe. She felt a sudden stab of fear. What state was the poor creature in?

Ben put his goggles on zoom. "I can't quite see it. It's half hidden behind the rocks."

They moved closer, stopped a short distance away from the panda and squatted down between two low boulders.

"I daren't look!" said Zoe.

"I'll do it," said Ben, peering over the rock in front of them. When he crouched back down again his face was solemn. He didn't want to have to tell his sister what he'd just seen.

CHAPTER SEVEN

"What's wrong?" asked Zoe. "Is he hurt?"

"That's not Jing Jing," said Ben slowly. "It's a wild panda."

"But it must be Jing Jing!" Zoe knelt up. At the foot of a sturdy tree trunk a few metres away, sat a huge adult panda. It was leaning casually against the tree, happily cleaning its belly. It was oblivious to the children. Zoe felt sick with despair. She'd been so sure they'd found the lost cub.

"There's one good thing," said Ben, trying to cheer her up. "That panda looked

healthy. It must have found another patch
of bamboo. Jing Jing's probably having a
slap-up meal right now." He hoped he
sounded more certain than he felt.

A ghostly cry filled the air.

"It's the leopard again," warned Ben.
"And it's close. Look at the panda."

The panda stopped cleaning, tilted its
head to one side and listened. Then it
scampered off into the undergrowth.

"The leopard won't be after us," insisted Zoe. "We've got no scent. But it might be tracking Jing Jing. He's young and weak – he'll be easy prey. Come on, we've got to keep searching. We saw Jing Jing's print so he must have been here recently. We've wasted so much time already."

She jumped up to scramble over the rock but slipped, banging her knee hard. She slumped to the ground with a yelp.

"You OK?" asked Ben.

"I'm fine," said Zoe, gritting her teeth as she rubbed her leg. "We're not stopping now."

"Yes we are," said Ben firmly. "It's too dangerous to go on tonight. We're worn out after that long walk up here and we've no idea if Jing Jing really is nearby. But what we do know is there's a leopard out there in the dark and scent or no scent, if it sees us, we'll look like dinner!"

"But we can't just leave Jing Jing to his fate." Ben could hear the wobble in Zoe's voice.

"What good would it do him if we fell down a ravine or ended up in the belly of a big cat?" he asked, catching hold of Zoe's arm. "Look, there's an overhang of rock by those pine trees. It makes a sort of cave. We can get some sleep and then search again in the morning. The scent dispersers should stop the leopard from tracking us."

Ben got out the sleeping bags and laid them on the forest floor, under the makeshift roof. "It's not going to get that cold overnight but we'll want some sort of covering and Erika said these are waterproof." He kicked aside piles of sharp pine needles. "Don't want these as a mattress though!" he added, laughing.

There were two of Mr Zhi's wraps left. Ben passed one to Zoe. "Eat," he ordered.

But Zoe only managed a few mouthfuls.

"I'm going to be awake all night," she told Ben, handing him the remainder of her food. "I'm too worried about Jing Jing." She climbed into her sleeping bag and stretched out, using her rucksack as a pillow.

"Do you want a drink?" asked Ben, holding out his water bottle.

There was no reply. Zoe was fast asleep.

Zoe suddenly woke with a start to find two eyes staring at her. She tried to move but something was pressing on her chest. Was it the clouded leopard? She could feel her heart thudding as the strange shape came slowly into focus in the pale dawn light.

A golden snub-nosed monkey was gawping down at her, its head on one side. Zoe burst out laughing in relief, sending the monkey squawking for cover.

"Whassgoingon?" Ben groaned and
opened his eyes. "I was in the middle of a
great dream. You were about to serve up a
nice cooked breakfast."

"You can have one of these." Zoe held up
a squashed Nutrobar. "Field rations," she
said with a grin. "Not the tastiest but they'll
stop our stomachs growling and frightening
off all the wildlife."

They sat on Ben's sleeping bag, munching
the rubbery fruit bars and swigging water to
wash them down. Birds overhead called to
each other with whistles and screeches.

"That'll stop me being hungry for about five minutes," said Ben. "Don't be surprised if I start gnawing at a tree or something."

Zoe rolled up her sleeping bag and checked her watch. "Six o'clock," she said. "On with the search." She peered out into the early morning mist. "If only we had an automatic panda finder!"

Ben couldn't help grinning. "Hang on," he said, pretending to search in his backpack, "I'm sure Uncle Stephen packed one for us."

Zoe gave him a shove. Ben shoved her back. Zoe rolled away giggling. Then she came to a sudden halt. She scrambled to her knees and peered closely at the ground.

"I've found another print," she gasped.

"Not falling for one of your tricks," said Ben smugly. "You're just trying to get me back."

"I wouldn't joke about this," insisted Zoe.

"Look!"

Keeping one eye on his sister and ready for any ambush, Ben crouched and inspected the ground. "A back pad and only three claws," he exclaimed. "We're on Jing Jing's trail again."

"Got another one," called Zoe from under a bush. "And another. They're fresh and they're heading for the waterfall."

"There's some tracks over here too," said Ben. "But they're certainly not panda. There are four toes and a roundish pad." He aimed his BUG at them. "Clouded leopard!" he exclaimed. "And heading in the same direction as Jing Jing."

Zoe joined him. "Looks like he's being stalked," she said grimly. "Let's hope we find him before the leopard does."

"I've thought of a good search pattern for us to follow," said Ben. "We'll check out the area round the pool in a semicircle, moving towards it as we go. That way we've got the best chance of homing in on him. He can't have climbed the sheer rock of the falls."

Using the BUG map to plot their course,

FOREST

PINE
TREES

ROCK

DEAD BAMBOO

Ben and Zoe advanced side by side through the forest, pushing aside ferns and bushes, and peering into all the shadowy places where a panda could hide.

WATERFALL

POOL

DENSE FOREST

N

STREAM

NOT TO SCALE

"What's that noise?" Zoe came to a sudden halt and listened intently.

Ben stopped next to her. "Sounds a bit like a small dog yapping," he said.

"They were playing animal cries just like that in the infomation room at the sanctuary," said Zoe, clutching Ben's arm. "You know, where we saw the photos of Jing Jing. They're from a panda."

Ben quickly pressed a key on his BUG to identify the call.

"We'll have to get closer," he said, holding it up as high as he could. "It's not picking them up from here."

"They're coming from that direction," said Zoe, setting off into the densest part of the forest.

"But we've already searched that area," Ben called after her.

"It can't have been calling then or we would have heard it." Zoe plunged into the dark undergrowth, pausing every now and again to check the direction of the sound. She turned to find Ben waving his BUG at her.

"You were right," he said. "I'm picking it up now. It is a panda."

As he spoke the call faded and stopped.

"Supposing we've scared him away," whispered Zoe.

"Or he's been attacked," added Ben, with a worried frown. "Though I haven't heard the leopard since last night."

They crept among the ferns and branches, trying not to crunch too loudly on the cones and twigs underfoot as they moved towards where the call had come from. Red-backed beetles and small spiders scuttled out of their path.

"Why can't we find him?" said Zoe. "He must be near here somewhere."

"You know what Gran says when we can't find something," said Ben. "You haven't looked properly."

"But we have," said Zoe. "Jing Jing's either gone or he's really well hidden." She delved into her backpack and slipped on the special thermogoggles that Erika had given them. "I wonder if we're near enough to use these."

Ben pulled his on and slowly scanned the area.

"Wow!" he exclaimed. "I didn't realize there was so much animal life around!" Through the glasses he could see the shapes of creatures moving through the forest, their bodies glowing purple, yellow and orange.

"Concentrate!" Zoe told him. "Can you see anything that looks like a panda?"

Ben shook his head. "Nothing yet. Monkeys of all sizes, parrots – they look really cool when they're flying and—"

"There's something big right over there," said Zoe, pointing. They both took off their glasses. "Behind that dead tree stump."

Watching and listening for every sound, the two children moved cautiously towards the tall, wide-girthed tree. When they reached it they slowly peeped round.

"Nothing there!" Zoe sighed.

"But the glasses can't be wrong," said Ben. He pulled his over his eyes again and checked around.

Then he stopped and stared hard at the trunk.

"There is something here," he whispered. "Something big. And it's right inside the tree!"

CHAPTER EIGHT

Ben fumbled for his torch but Zoe quickly pulled him back away from the stump. "Better be careful. It could be anything – we've heard leopard calls, don't forget."

There was a sudden movement from the dead tree. Ben and Zoe ripped off their goggles and took cover at a distance.

"Round black ears!" said Ben in a whisper. "That's no leopard."

"White face," Zoe whispered back as the top of a furry head appeared. "It's definitely a panda! It's got to be Jing Jing this time!"

"Don't get your hopes up," murmured Ben as two black eye patches slowly appeared.

"It looks like a cub," breathed Zoe, watching the slow-moving animal intently. "If it is Jing Jing I reckon he's hiding from the leopard in there."

The panda climbed clumsily out of its hole, grunting painfully as it moved. It plopped to the ground and rested against the tree, slowly turning its head, scanning the dense forest. Its ears twitched as if it was listening.

"Let's get a bit nearer," Ben whispered in Zoe's ear. "If it's Jing Jing he won't be scared. He's used to people."

Their hearts in their mouths, they moved towards the young panda.

At first the cub didn't stir. It gazed from one to the other, panting heavily.

"It looks undernourished," whispered Ben. "No round belly. And its eyes are dull."

"Don't be scared," said Zoe, kneeling down in front of the little panda. "We won't hurt you." She looked up at Ben. "I can't see its back paws. We still don't know if it's Jing Jing."

Ben slid a hand into his backpack. "Jing Jing or not, it needs our help."

He broke off a piece of panda bread and handed it to Zoe. Flinching at the movement, the panda suddenly scrambled to its feet. The next moment it had disappeared among the trees.

"That must have been a wild panda too," said Ben. "Jing Jing wouldn't have been frightened like that."

"It was Jing Jing," said Zoe, jumping up. "I saw his paw as he went. It only had three toes."

"Then why did he run away?" said Ben.

"I think it might be the scent dispersers," Zoe reminded him. "We might have looked like humans but we wouldn't have smelt right. That would've confused him. And he's been alone in the forest for some time now. He'll be scared of everything. Anyway, don't argue! Follow me. The tracks are really clear. And they're heading back to the dead bamboo."

They followed the line of tracks downhill through the brown withered stalks. At first it led in a straight line, then the steps seemed to waiver.

"I reckon it was just adrenalin giving him the energy to run away," said Ben, as they examined the faltering prints. "He can't be far now. He'll be more exhausted than ever, an easy target for the leopard."

"We've got to get to him first," muttered Zoe as they tiptoed forwards. "But this time we take it really slowly. No sudden movements – and scent dispersers off."

They could hear the waterfall crashing in the distance somewhere up above them. At last the trees thinned a little and the prints led to a narrow stream.

Something was moving on the other side amongst the ferns. It was taking slow labouring steps, stopping every now and then to muster enough energy to carry on.

Then it stopped abruptly and slumped to the ground.

"There he is!" breathed Ben. "We've found him. Now remember, no sudden movements."

"He's shivering," said Zoe, peering out. "He must be cold. Come on, we need to cross over to him."

"He's not cold," said Ben, and Zoe could hear tension in his voice. "He's afraid. Stay absolutely still."

"What's the matter?"

"Up there."

Zoe followed his gaze. Crouched on a branch above Jing Jing was a snarling clouded leopard. Its coat, dark and blotched like a snake, rippled as its muscles tensed.

"It's going to pounce!" she gasped in horror.

But the leopard's head suddenly whipped round, its ears twitching wildly.

"What's the matter with it?" whispered Ben.

The forest all around came alive with anxious bird calls and monkey cries and the leopard gave a strange high-pitched yowl. Without another look at the panda, it streaked off and was gone.

RRRUMMBBBLE! A deafening sound rose from under them as if rocks were being hurled together. The ground began to shake. With a tremendous flutter of wings the birds left the trees and distant cries of terrified animals filled the forest. Zoe was thrown off her feet. She crashed into Ben and they both went sprawling.

"Curl up!" Ben shouted. Zoe didn't need telling twice. She made herself into a tight ball, head covered. Ben dived down next to her, uphill of her body, his backpack between them and the falling rocks.

Stones and small boulders were tumbling down the hill, bouncing over them. Ben could feel the impact of them striking his backpack, which cushioned the heavy blows.

And then as suddenly as it had started, the rumbling stopped.

"Thanks, Ben," said Zoe gratefully. "That was quick thinking."

"And that was some aftershock!" gasped Ben.

Zoe scrambled to her feet. "Where's Jing Jing?" she cried in alarm, scanning the forest. "I can't see him."

"It's all right," said Ben. "He's taken shelter by that bush over there."

The little panda lay under the overhanging leaves, his head slumped down on his chest.

"We must get to him," said Zoe, urgently tugging at Ben's arm.

"Too right," agreed Ben. "He's barely moving. Perhaps he was hurt by the falling rocks. And we don't know if the leopard's still around."

They were about to jump across the narrow stream when more rumbling filled the air.

"What's that?" cried Zoe, stopping suddenly. "Is it another aftershock?"

"The ground's not shaking this time." Ben peered up the slope of the mountain. "It's coming from the direction of the waterfall. It's as if the hill's roaring."

A noise like an explosion battered their ears as water burst out from the slope above, flattening trees and bushes in its wake. It surged down the hillside in a deafening torrent, bringing earth, rocks and branches with it. Ben and Zoe stumbled back in terror away from the wall of water that pounded into the narrow stream. More rocks were falling now and whole trees were slipping down the slope towards them. Ben pulled Zoe further back from the shifting earth.

"The aftershock's done this!" gasped Ben, as a huge boulder went crashing past. "It must've blocked the underground river. Now all the water's coming this way."

Horrified, Ben and Zoe gazed down the steep, sloping bank at their feet. Below them the wide, raging river, bulging with rocks and wood, rushed wildly downhill. Jing Jing lay unmoving under his umbrella of branches on the opposite side. The ground was much lower there and the water was sucking away at the bank. He was within centimetres of the deadly flow.

"If the earth crumbles any further he'll be swept away," Zoe whispered. "And there's no way we can get across to him."

CHAPTER NINE

"He's not going to be swept away if I can help it," said Ben, a look of grim determination on his face. "What can we use to make a bridge?"

"There are uprooted trees everywhere," said Zoe. "But they'd all be too heavy to move."

Ben gave a hollow laugh. "If we were Tarzan we could swing across."

"We can't swing across," said Zoe, her eyes shining, "but we can zip wire. Our bank's higher than Jing Jing's and Uncle Stephen gave us those Fisher Integrated

Nanofirers, remember?" She pulled her FIN out of her backpack. "Erika told me about it on the plane. You were meant to be listening too. There's a nanocord inside."

"Those really strong cords that are only a few atoms thick?" said Ben eagerly. "I thought scientists were still developing them."

"Uncle Stephen's ahead of the game," said Zoe.

"Sounds great, but how are we going to see a cord that thin?"

"It glows," said Zoe impatiently. "And before you ask I don't know how and we haven't got time to find out."

She peered across the river. "We just need something to secure the cord on both sides. Tree trunks should be fine. That one over there just beyond Jing Jing looks strong. Erika said there's a dart on the end of the cord. The FIN will shoot it into the wood and hold the wire firm."

She aimed the bulb end of the torch-like gadget over the river and squeezed the tube. A dart whizzed out of the FIN and sped across the raging torrent, carrying a red glowing wire after it. The dart missed the tree and tangled itself in the bushes. Zoe pressed the button marked R and it instantly retracted like an automatic tape measure.

"I'll do it," said Ben, reaching out.

"No!" insisted Zoe. She shot again. This time the dart embedded itself in the trunk. Zoe reached up and banged the other end of the FIN hard against the tree behind her. There was a thud as something inside it rammed into the bark. "That's locked it in position. Now we can zip wire down it."

"Brilliant!" exclaimed Ben. "And I've worked out what this hook's for on the top of my backpack." Zoe recognized the gleam in his eye that meant he was going to do something impulsive. Ben tightened his backpack round him. Then he reached behind his head, grasped the little metal hook and clipped himself to the wire. "See you on the other side!"

"Wait!" cried Zoe in alarm. "We haven't tested it."

"No time!" Ben replied, kicking off. "Wahoo!" She heard him yell above the roaring water.

Ben sped down the wire, his backpack acting as a harness. His feet skimmed the river, which sucked and bubbled as it plunged down the mountainside. He braced himself as the tree sped towards him. *Thump!* He felt the jolt right through his body.

He reached up, unclipped his backpack from the wire and dropped to the ground.

Then he ran to the panda. Jing Jing didn't move. He didn't even seem to be breathing.

Ben saw Zoe flash past and heard her exclamation as she slammed into the tree behind him.

"Jing Jing." Zoe knelt down beside the panda cub, stroking his head. "We've come to take you home. He's so cold," she whispered. "Are we too late?" She looked at Ben, her eyes filling with tears.

Jing Jing suddenly gave a ragged breath.

"He's alive!" she gasped. "Quick, put some water into his feeding bottle and pass it over."

Ben thrust the bottle into Zoe's hand. She put the teat to Jing Jing's pale lips. At first nothing happened. Then Jing Jing's eyes slowly opened. His mouth began to close feebly round the teat.

"Go on, Jing Jing," urged Zoe. "Drink."

The panda took a spluttering mouthful, and another. Then with faint grunts he began to gulp down the water.

Zoe gently eased the bottle from his mouth. "Not too much at once! Your body's not used to it."

Suddenly the bank at their feet began to crumble away, battered by the force of the water. Ben and Zoe leaped up and took Jing Jing by the front legs. They pulled with all their strength and just managed to drag him away from the edge in time. The ground where he'd been sitting was swept downriver.

"That was close!" panted Ben. "Jing Jing may be starving but he still weighs a lot. We're never going to manage to carry him down the mountain. We must contact Uncle Stephen straight away." He touched the BUG hot key that would get them straight through to Wild HQ.

Jing Jing lay on the ground, trembling. Zoe helped him to sit up, tucking her sleeping bag behind him. She got out some panda bread, soaked it in the water and touched it to his lips. But the panda cub didn't seem to notice.

"What news?" Uncle Stephen's voice burst out.

"We've located Jing Jing!" Ben called into the speaker.

"Good work!" Uncle Stephen sounded delighted.

"He's very weak," Ben reported. "And we can't transport him back to Ningshang."

"Not surprised," came their godfather's voice. "He'll weigh as much as you! Don't worry, I can work out your coordinates from your transmission. I'll let the sanctuary know where to find him – anonymously, of course. Just make sure they don't see you when they get there. Over and out."

Ben squatted beside Jing Jing. "Now all we can do is keep our little friend alive – and wait."

"Remember how long it took us to get up here?" said Zoe anxiously. "The rescuers are going to be ages." She offered the panda another drink. He lifted his head and feebly

tried to clasp the bottle between his front
paws. Then his head flopped back down.

"But they know exactly where to come,"
Ben reminded her. "They won't be wasting
time searching like we did."

Zoe suddenly stiffened. "We've got
company," she said, pointing across the river.

The clouded leopard was prowling up and
down the opposite bank, watching them
intently.

Ben and Zoe sat perfectly still.

"I know it can't get to us," whispered Zoe. "But it's scary even so."

"Do you think it's been after Jing Jing all this time?" asked Ben.

"I don't know," said Zoe. "I'm just glad we got to him first."

"I'm just glad we've got a raging torrent to protect us."

The leopard stopped its pacing and cautiously made its way down to the water as if looking for a way across.

"Surely it won't try and swim?" gasped Zoe.

The leopard seemed to think about it, then backed away from the rushing river. It stared at them for a moment and slowly slunk off until it was just a shadow in the undergrowth. After a moment it was gone.

Ben and Zoe sat either side of Jing Jing trying to keep him warm as they waited for the sanctuary to arrive. The little panda's breathing was shallow now and his tongue was lolling out.

Ben suddenly jumped to his feet, waving his BUG screen at his sister. "Look at this – the satellite map has updated itself. This water's made a wide landslip right down into the valley and over to the river. The rescuers might get here in time but they'll be on the other side."

The horror of their predicament hit Zoe.

"Then there's no way the rescuers can get to Jing Jing," she gasped.

CHAPTER TEN

"Don't give up, boy!" Zoe whispered, tucking the warm sleeping bag round Jing Jing. "We'll think of something."

"We have to get back to the other side," muttered Ben.

"No way!" gasped his sister. "The leopard could return at any time!"

"We'll just have to risk it."

"Even if we could get across we'd never manage to take Jing Jing over with us," insisted Zoe. "We've got to stay here, Ben."

But Ben was deep in thought. "Pity we

can't zip wire uphill – or can we?" He
jumped to his feet. "I've still got my FIN!"

"Yes, but I don't see—"

"We can go back the way we came." Ben
flung everything out of his backpack until
he found the torch-like gadget. He aimed it
across the river and up at the tree where
Zoe's FIN was already bolted. The dart
zipped over the water, and settled deep in
the trunk.

"I'm a better shot than you!" said Ben,
testing the glowing cord with a tug.

"Beginner's luck," muttered Zoe. "And
you haven't thought this through. Now
we've got two uphill cords to get us – and
a heavy panda – across to the other side.
It can't be done."

"Yes it can," declared Ben. "We make a
sling for Jing Jing with rope and a sleeping
bag and attach it to your nanocord. We
both climb on with him. Then I tie this

end of my FIN on to the sling and press
retract. That should pull us across. Watch."
Ben pressed the R button. Immediately he
was jerked forward on to his stomach and
dragged towards the river as the cord
retracted. Zoe shouted in alarm. Ben
frantically pressed the switch again, the
cord stopped pulling and he came to a halt,
right on the edge of the fierce flow.

"Well, I've proved it's powerful," he said shakily as he stood up and backed away from the bank, playing the nanocord out again as he went. He bent down and gave Jing Jing a gentle pat. "You're going to have a zip ride, my friend."

"Hope it works," muttered Zoe, pulling Ben's sleeping bag out of his backpack and laying it on the ground under the zip wire.

With a lot of puffing and panting they managed to roll Jing Jing's dead weight on to the bag. He hardly stirred.

Ben got two ropes from his backpack, threaded one through the two eyelets in the top corners of the sleeping bag and the second through the eyelets at the bottom.

"Now we have to tie the ropes over the nanocord," he said. "You take the top and I'll take the bottom. That will hoist him up off the ground. Ready? Pull."

Soon Jing Jing was suspended above the

ground in his makeshift sling. Ben climbed on at the front, next to the panda cub's head.

"You go at his feet," he told his sister, as he tied the strap of his FIN firmly to one of the sling ropes. Zoe climbed on behind and gripped hard. The sling rocked with her weight, but the ropes held.

"Are you sure about this, Ben?" said Zoe. "We might all end up in the river."

"It's Jing Jing's only chance," insisted Ben. "Hang on tightly to the ropes – and here we go!" He pressed the retract button.

They were jerked forwards as the nanocord wound itself back inside the gadget and pulled the sling along.

"It's working!" he shouted. "Keep holding on, Zoe."

With the FIN whirring madly, they found themselves being pulled out over the tumbling water as the nanocord retracted.

Zoe glanced down at the fierce foam. It made her feel sick to think of them plummeting down into the fast flowing torrent below. She gripped tightly to the sling ropes and kept her eyes firmly on the bank opposite.

"Nearly there!" Ben shouted to his sister at last.

They were almost over the bank when they felt a sudden jolt.

"What's happened?" cried Zoe in alarm. "We've stopped!"

Ben pressed the retract button again and again. "It's broken," he called. "My nanocord's stopped glowing. We're stuck."

"Could you jump to the bank from here?" Zoe shouted back. "Then you can pull us the rest of the way."

"I'll try." Ben eased himself round to face the bank.

"Be careful!"

Ben crouched. As he launched himself over the water he knew he wasn't going to make it. He half jumped, half fell towards the high bank. His legs plunged into the water. The cold current sucked at him as he clutched desperately at a tangled root. He kicked out and managed to get his knees into a hole in the bank. At last he hauled himself up and collapsed, breathless.

"Ben!" Zoe was calling and her voice sounded strange. Ben looked up. The clouded leopard was back. It was crouched on the bank, scarcely a metre away.

Belly on the ground, it began to slink slowly
and deliberately towards him.

Ben's heart was beating so fast he thought
it would burst out of his chest. Any
moment now the leopard was going to leap
– and there was nothing he could do about
it. Or was there? He snatched up a stone
and flung it hard at the beast. It flinched
back as the stone struck the ground in front
of it, sending up a shower of earth. Then it
tensed, ready to pounce.

Suddenly the air was filled with a tremendous roar. The leopard whipped round, its ears twitching wildly. Horrified, Ben followed its gaze.

"It can't be…" he whispered.

A huge tiger was standing a metre from them, its teeth bared.

The leopard gave a yowl of terror and was gone.

And then, to Ben's utter astonishment, the tiger shimmered and disappeared. Confused, he looked over to Zoe. And then he understood. She was holding her BUG and directing it towards where the tiger had been.

"It was a holo-image!" he gasped. "Of course it had to be. South China tigers are practically extinct in the wild. There certainly aren't any in this region any more. Good job the leopard didn't know that. Brilliant, Zoe. You saved my life."

"Well, in return perhaps you'd like to get us to the bank," said Zoe, clambering round to the front of the sling. Holding tightly to the rope with one hand, she stretched out the other towards Ben.

"It's no good," she said. "I can't reach you."

Ben looked about the bank and picked up a sturdy branch. "Get hold of this," he called. Zoe made a grab for the stick but her fingers slipped down the wet wood. Ben thrust it out again and this time Zoe managed to grip it tightly. Ben pulled with all his strength. Slowly the sling began to move forwards until it was hovering over the bank, just a few centimetres from the ground. Zoe jumped down and helped Ben untie the ropes. The sling bumped to the ground and Jing Jing rolled out with a faint groan.

"We made it!" exclaimed Zoe. "I just hope Jing Jing's all right."

As she bent down to the panda cub there
was a sudden shout from the forest.

Ben and Zoe looked at each other.
"Quick! We've got to hide!" said Ben
urgently.

"And conceal all evidence," added Zoe,
twisting her FIN to eject it from the tree.
She held the two buttons down. The dart
on the other side of the river was released
and her cord flew back into her gizmo. But
Ben's was still dead.

"There's no way we can cut this
nanocord," he said. "I'm going to have to
ditch my FIN." He slung the gizmo high up
into the tree. Now there was no sign of it.

They snatched up their backpacks and
the sleeping bag and dived into the bushes
just as someone in a blue sanctuary
sweatshirt burst on to the bank. She
shouted something in Sichuanese.

"Put your translator in!" Zoe hissed to Ben.

"Jing Jing's here!" they heard the woman shout.

Three men and a second woman ran up and knelt down next to Jing Jing, dropping their bags to the ground.

"He's still alive!" Someone opened a medical box.

"But only just. His pulse is weak."

"Wonder who sent that message." One of the workers scanned the trees. Ben and Zoe shrunk back into the shadows. "There's no one around."

"No questions, the man said, remember! The main thing is we've got to him in time."

Very soon the little panda was being gently eased on to a stretcher. A drip with a bag of clear fluid was attached to one leg. A woman stood beside the stretcher, holding the bag up.

At last the rescue party disappeared,

carefully carrying the panda cub back home. Ben and Zoe crept out from their hiding place.

"Jing Jing's in good hands now," said Zoe softly. "I think he's going to make it."

CHAPTER ELEVEN

Ben and Zoe emerged from the forest in to the sunshine. They were near the site of the new medical centre and beyond they could just see the roof of their hotel. Behind them, the landslide water plunged down the hill on its way to meet the river.

Ben's BUG vibrated. "It's Uncle Stephen!"

"Hello there!" Their godfather's voice came out loud and clear. "Any news?"

"The sanctuary people made it up the mountain," Zoe reported. "We're on our way now to check on Jing Jing."

"I told you they're a good lot at Ningshang," said Uncle Stephen.

"But what did you tell them?" asked Ben. "I mean, who did you say you were?"

"I said, hello there, I'm Dr Fisher, head of a top secret organization... " They gasped and heard their godfather chuckling away. "No, don't worry. I hinted that I was something to do with the government and that they'd better ask no questions. I didn't want to scare anyone but I had to make sure they took me seriously. Anyway … cheerio."

"Our godfather has some strange ideas sometimes," said Zoe with a grin.

"But they seem to work!" added Ben, pocketing his BUG.

"I can't believe how tired I am," groaned Zoe. "My legs have never ached so much."

"What do you expect?" Ben laughed. "We've walked for miles, narrowly missed a landslide, got stuck on a zip wire, escaped from a leopard and rescued a panda." He looked slyly at his sister. "So you're too tired to go to the sanctuary and find out how Jing Jing's doing?"

Zoe's eyes sparkled. "Course not!" she exclaimed. "Race you."

Laughing, they ran down the slope.

They were soon at the gate of the sanctuary.

"I've just had a dreadful thought," said Zoe, pulling at Ben's sleeve. "Do you think

Xu Mei will want to see us? We weren't her favourite people yesterday."

"Let's just go and ask about Jing Jing and see what happens," said Ben.

A man was coming towards them carrying buckets of vegetables.

"Excuse me," called Zoe. "We were wondering if the little panda has been found?"

The man looked them up and down, a shocked expression on his face.

Ben and Zoe suddenly realized how dirty and dishevelled they were. Zoe pulled a twig out of Ben's hair.

"Er ... we fell down a hole," said Ben lamely.

The man put down his buckets and scratched his head. "I not understand," he said at last. "My English not good…"

"Jing Jing?" Zoe prompted him.

"Ah yes ... he is…"

"Zoe! Ben!" A happy cry came across from the infirmary. It was Xu Mei and she was beaming from ear to ear. "Jing Jing's back and he's going to be all right."

The man motioned for them to go and they ran over to her. She grabbed their hands and took them inside the building. They had to make their way past an area of rubble and tarpaulin where the wall was damaged.

Xu Mei led them to a room at the end. She knocked on the door and stuck her head inside. They heard some gabbled Chinese but didn't pick up what was being said. Then the door opened wide and Xu Mei's father stood there.

"Come in." He beamed. "Meet our naughty cub."

A woman was leaning over a large plastic cot. There, lying on a blanket and with the tube still in his leg, lay Jing Jing. At once Zoe and Ben could see there was

more life in his eyes. He was sucking
noisily at a bottle of milk. As soon as he
caught sight of them he gave an excited
little squeak.

"He thinks you're his friends," said Xu Mei.

"He looks a lot better than… " began
Zoe. Ben coughed loudly. "…better than I
expected him to," she gabbled.

"He's getting water and food in the drip,"
said Xu Mei. "Father doesn't want him
eating too quickly. His stomach has shrunk
and it will make him sick. But he loves his
milk so much that we couldn't say no to a
little bit."

They stayed at the panda's side, stroking
his ears, while he gulped down his milk.
Then his eyes grew heavy, the bottle fell to
his side and he began to snore.

"A good sleep," said Zoe. "Just what he
needs."

Xu Mei nodded. "We leave him now."

Out in the corridor, Zoe took Xu Mei's hand. "I hope you've forgiven us for not going into the mountains with you yesterday."

The little girl looked at her gravely. "I was silly. It was too dangerous for children to go up there."

"It certainly was," said Ben, catching his sister's eye.

"If only I knew who found Jing Jing," Xu Mei went on. "I could say thank you."

"I'm sure his rescuers know how grateful you are," said Zoe.

Suddenly Xu Mei stared intently at their filthy clothes.

"I was just thinking," she said, her eyes shining. "Jing Jing did his happy cry when he saw you. It was like he had met you before."

"But that's impossible," said Ben, "isn't it?"

"Yes." Xu Mei nodded. A huge smile spread over her face. "Impossible."

They peered through the glass door of the infirmary. Jing Jing lay peacefully asleep in his cot.

Xu Mei sighed happily.

"There's one thing his rescuers can be sure of," said Zoe, smiling. "Jing Jing is the best loved panda in the whole world."

WILD

GIANT PANDA SURVIVAL

Giant pandas were once widespread across southern and eastern China, Myanmar and North Vietnam. Now they are only found in the wild in South West China.

No. of giant pandas living in the wild today ⟶ about 16,000
No. of these living in protected reserves ⟶ about 1,000
No. of giant pandas living in zoos ⟶ about 160

Life span: About 20 years in the wild • More than 30 in captivity
Oldest panda recorded – 37 years old

The giant panda is called the giant cat bear in China.

Weight: Adult pandas weigh between 80 and 150 kg. 150kg is about the weight of two average men. The male panda is generally a little larger than the female. Amazingly, a panda cub is very tiny at birth. It weighs only about 140g – a little heavier than a newborn kitten.

STATUS: ENDANGERED

The giant panda is on the red list of the International Union for Conservation of Nature, who says that its numbers are declining.

RESCUE

GIANT PANDA FACTS

THREATS

DEFORESTATION

Giant pandas live in a few high mountainous areas that have natural forested areas with fir, spruce and bamboo. These areas are threatened by logging, mining and road building. Destruction of their habitat is now the major threat to their survival. In the eleven years from 1973 to 1984, it shrank by 50 per cent.

Poaching has declined thanks to tough laws. A poacher can receive a prison sentence of up to ten years. However, pandas sometimes get caught in traps intended for other animals such as musk deer and black bears.

STARVATION

When bamboo flowers it dies down and takes about 20 years to grow again. This can cause severe food shortage for pandas.

LOW REPRODUCTON

It has been difficult to breed giant pandas in captivity. They do not adapt easily to the presence of humans.

PREDATORS

Jackals and leopards prey on adult pandas.

It's not all bad news!

By mid-2005, the Chinese government had established over 50 panda reserves protecting more than 4,000 square miles of forest – nearly half the remaining giant panda habitat. Efforts are being made to plant bamboo corridors to link bamboo areas for the wild pandas. Breeding success is gradually increasing as scientists learn more about how to make the giant pandas' captive environment more natural.

Twins Ben and Zoe are devastated at being left at home when their parents head to Africa for their next veterinary adventure. But they're about to have an adventure of their own. Contacted by renowned zoologist Dr Stephen Fisher, they are recruited into Wild. Soon the children are on their way to Sumatra to rescue a tiger and her two cubs from a gang of vicious poachers...

J. BURCHETT & S. VOGLER

WILD RESCUE

FOREST FIRE

Ben and Zoe's latest mission takes them to South Borneo. An orang-utan has set up home on a palm oil plantation and is resisting all attempts to bring him to the safety of the nearby reservation. But when they discover that illegal logging has been taking place, it becomes clear that the orang-utan isn't the only one in grave danger.

Following reports of a polar bear found dead near an Alaskan village, Uncle Stephen is sending Ben and Zoe to investigate. It is highly unusual for the animals to be found so close to human habitation. But the mission takes another turn when Ben and Zoe learn that the dead bear had recently given birth. This means there is an orphaned cub out there. Will they find it in time?

If you want to find out
more about pandas visit:

www.panda.org.cn/english
www.wwf.org.uk